Celebrate Family
Lisa DosSantos

Mango Tree Press, P.O. Box 853, Mackinaw City, MI 49701
(231).627.7322
www.mangotreepress.com

ISBN 0-9708571-1-X
Library of Congress Control Number 2004103379

T 54873

With special thanks to
Michael North
I am truly indebted.
L.D.S.

and

Pam Yell
A Step Above Copies
L.D.S. & K.B.

Especially for Pa and John

We hope you are proud.

And to all the Grandpas of the Mighty Mackinac Bridge
You have our respect and gratitude.

"Charlie Birch, will you please slow it down!"  Charlie heard his Grandma's voice from the kitchen as the screen door slammed behind him.

Although it was still the first week of May, the weather in Mackinaw City was already quite warm.  With the door open, Charlie could smell the chocolate chip cookies his Grandma was baking even before he set foot in the house.  Could she really blame him for running?  After all, it was Friday afternoon and that meant no school for two whole days.  Time to play!

"Here Charlie, sit down and tell me about your day. How is the fourth grade treating you?" Grandma inquired.

"It's OK," Charlie provided as he jumped up on the kitchen stool. "I really like math. Mr. Selnick is really cool. But I don't know about history. It's so boring and I have a report due in two weeks," Charlie managed to get out between bites of Grandma's perfectly perfect cookies.

Reaching for a second, Charlie asked with anticipation, "Well, where is he? How is he feeling today?"

Grandma hesitated. "On the back porch…as usual, staring at that bridge, still feeling a little gloomy, I think."

"Well, I'm sure one of these will cheer him up," Charlie said, already on his feet and out the door with enough cookies in hand for himself and his Grandpa.

As Charlie approached the porch, he heard the music that filled the air wherever Grandpa was - the unmistakable sound of the greatest entertainer that ever lived - Al Jolson.  The music took some getting used to, but Charlie enjoyed it now.  He really enjoyed how it made his Grandpa happy.

There he was, rocking in the chair, toes tapping almost automatically because he was most likely also half asleep.

"Grandpa!  Hey wake up!  It's me, and I have some of Grandma's cookies," Charlie coaxed.

"Sonny boy," Grandpa jolted up. "It's good to see you today.  And I wasn't sleeping, you know."

"I know.  How are you feeling?  Grandma said you've been a little down."

"Oh, your Grandma worries too much," Grandpa said as he rustled the hair on Charlie's head.  "Now, didn't you say you had a cookie for me?"

The two enjoyed their snacks, the warm afternoon sun and a little guy time.

Charlie just adored his Grandpa. He loved to listen to stories of how life was when he was a boy living in Mackinaw. How he helped his own parents run Friendly Folks, the fudge and souvenir shop that Charlie's parents now operate. How he rode his red Schwinn bicycle all over town, sometimes as far as French Farm and Spruce Ridge out near Wilderness Park.

He especially enjoyed listening to his Grandpa tell stories of how he helped build the Mighty Mac, one of the longest suspension bridges in the whole world.

Lately, however, Grandpa hasn't been himself. He hasn't wanted to play cards. He hasn't wanted to go fishing. He hasn't even wanted to take the boat out on Lake Huron. Despite all efforts, not even Charlie could figure out what was wrong.

"What do you say we take the boat out for a little spin?" Charlie asked. "It's a beautiful day and the water is so calm," he encouraged.

"Not today my sonny boy. Maybe another time," Grandpa replied as he reached down to pat his second favorite guy, his dog, on the behind. "Why don't you take George here for a walk down on the shore? He needs a little exercise. You'd be doing me a favor."

The word 'walk' was all George had to hear. He was up and ready to go before Charlie could answer. "All right," he said, "but it won't be the same without you."

Charlie slapped the side of his leg. "C'mon George, let's go. In an instant the stocky Bassett Hound was right on Charlie's heel, ready to dip his paws in the cool, crisp Lake Huron water.

All around Charlie were the sights and sounds of spring in northern Michigan. The sky was bluer than on any day he could remember. The ferry boats were transporting tourists to and from Mackinac Island. The summer season was fast approaching and soon Mackinaw City would be bustling with people visiting from all over. Seagulls flew overhead, swooping down occasionally to beg for any small morsel from unsuspecting people enjoying a meal at a picnic table.

Charlie spent some time trying to skip stones. "How does Grandpa get these things to sail so far?" he wondered out loud. As if to answer, George let out a big howl. "Yeah," Charlie agreed, "he's pretty cool, isn't he?"

Charlie and George tired each other out. After giving up on the stones, they played a serious game of fetch with a small fallen tree branch, then tug of war with a forgotten beach towel.

Completely exhausted, they got cozy on a small spot of sand, took deep refreshing breaths and proceeded to fall deeply asleep.

When Charlie awoke, he felt groggy.  As he stood up, he rubbed his eyes, gave his body a head-to-toe stretch and let out an enormous yawn.

"Ah," he thought to himself, "there sure is nothing like a good nap." But as Charlie continued to stretch and wake up, instead of feeling more awake and alert, he began to feel more confused. No amount of eye rubbing could change what he saw.

As Charlie looked around, he noticed some extremely strange things. The automobiles, all of them, were like those seen only in the antique car shows his Grandpa liked to go to every summer in St. Ignace.  And the people, well, they were straight off the set of a 1950's movie.

Things were looking more like a page from a local history book than what he knew they should be.

While Charlie's good sense told him to run as fast as he could back to his Grandparent's house, the sound of drums and trumpets and cheers coming from Central Avenue aroused his curiosity. Unable to resist, he followed the music and found himself running down the main street of Mackinaw City, searching for signs of something familiar. He saw his family's store, except now it looked like the pictures his Grandma kept in her scrapbook. Not much else looked the way it should either.

Charlie's head was swimming. He ran faster than those marching in the parade. He needed to find out where they were going and what in the world was happening.

He pushed his way through the crowds, nearly out of breath and more tired now than when he had lain down for a nap. Charlie met with the end of the parade, ironically, just where he had awakened a short time before: at the foot of the bridge, or to be exact, where the bridge should have been.

The Mighty Mac was not there! Simply put, the bridge, the whole bridge, was gone!

"OK," Charlie said aloud. "Wake up." He gave himself a hard pinch. "Ouch!" That hurt.

Before Charlie had time to think, he heard someone's voice boom over a loud speaker. Although he couldn't hear every word, from where he stood he caught bits and pieces.

"Welcome all. On this beautiful day, we begin…they said it couldn't be built … engineering marvel … hard work, dedication …"

As jets flew overhead, Charlie was patted on the back by a man standing next to him. "This is a day we'll never forget kid. May 8, 1954. Yes sirree, we'll remember this day forever."

May 8, 1954?
With that Charlie fell backwards into the crowd of people.

And now, in this strange reality of Charlie's, time would pass in a way it never had before.

Oh sure, the sun would rise in the morning and set at night. Northern Lights would dance across the sky.

Summer would follow spring. After the colors of autumn had fallen from the trees, winter's cold wind would spread its blanket of white, making all things frigid in the Straits of Mackinac.

Charlie didn't understand what was happening and almost didn't want to, for it looked as though Charlie Birch was about to become a part of history in the making.

The next thing he knew, there were voices, and faint shadows of men standing over him.

"Hey kid, wake up.  This is no place for a young boy to be napping. Where did you come from?" a familiar voice asked.

As his vision began to clear, his eyes met with a likewise familiar face. "No, it can't be," he mumbled.  "None of this can be."

"Oh yes it can," said another man. "Here it comes, right on schedule: the first caisson making its way from Rockport more than 90 miles away. This bridge is goin' up!"

That statement made all the guys take notice.  Their shift was over.  Their bodies felt as though they had been beaten.  Their feet were throbbing in their work boots.  They were sweating up a storm.  Their bellies were empty. Still, they could hardly wait to get back to work.  What man wouldn't want to be part of this - the challenge, the satisfaction of a good day's work, the honor, and hey, the money?

"It looks like Paul Bunyan's donut," Charlie said, looking out at Lake Huron as the extremely large caisson came into sight.  All the men laughed.

"It sure does kid," said a man as he grabbed his lunch pail from the roof of his car and tossed his hardhat onto the front seat.  "See you guys tomorrow. And J.B., you are leaving aren't you?"  This made the men laugh even harder.

"Yes, I'm going home," answered that familiar voice next to Charlie, "but I'll see you guys first thing in the morning."

The men said their good-byes, and before turning to walk away, J.B. patted Charlie on the head.  "You'd better get going home too, kid.  It's getting late and your folks will be worried."

"Sure," Charlie said. "I will."

George moaned and growled ever so softly in his sleep.  He must have been chasing the neighbor's cat again.  Charlie, too, rustled around. He was having the strangest dream…

The work continued.  The men pressed on and the bridge slowly took shape.  Turbulent waters crashed upon the shore, sculpting the strangest forms out of ice during the winter months.  Gale-force winds blew through the layers of clothing the men wore.  Temperatures fell and rose again.  Fog rolled through.

And Charlie saw and felt it all.

There was the forging of steel into massive structures by man and machine.

Hardworking men formed an honorable brotherhood unified by a common goal.

There was faith.

A belief that all things are possible, even the seemingly impossible.

There was bravery.
Remarkable heroism arose from confidence in self and one another.

There was invention; unmistakable human ingenuity.

And dedication and courage to build the bridge that couldn't be built.

"Well guys, look at her.  She's a beauty isn't she?  And none of us are any worse for the wear."

Charlie once again became aware of the men in his presence.  And that voice, how he wished he could place that voice.

"Are you here again kid?  You can't seem to get enough of this either. You want to go up there on one of those towers?" asked one of the men.

Charlie perked up like a hunting dog catching the scent of its prey. "Wow, could I?"

"Don't tease the boy," J.B. advised evenly.  "That's not nice.  Can't you see the want in his eyes?"

The other men laughed.  "J.B., we'll meet you at the Hungry Bear?"

"Sure guys.  I'll be right behind you."

While the other guys jumped in their cars to head over to the local after-work hang out, J.B., instead, sat down next to Charlie.

"Listen kid, maybe someday you'll get up there.  But today isn't going to be the day," J.B. offered.

"Then tell me what it's like," Charlie begged.  "You guys aren't afraid of anything."

"Oh, I don't know about that.  If there's fear, you don't think about it.  One thing is for sure – it's dangerous work and we're always aware of that.  That's what keeps us safe.  From day one it's been about getting down to business.  And us men joke around a lot down here, off the clock.  But you can be sure, when we put these here hardhats on, it's time to set the mind to the job and look out for the guy next to ya.  We trust each other with our lives up there.  J.B. paused.

"Look at that bridge over there.  It's been built to stand up to all forces of nature; the strong currents, high winds, ice and snow of these Straits.  It's all been done by determined, hardworking men.  You see that man over there?  That's Dr. Steinman.  He's here giving his brain-child the once-over.  There's a smart man.  He designed the Mighty Mac and some guys mined dolomite on Drummond Island, divers went down into that cold water, we ironworkers did our part, the laborers did theirs and those guys up there now are laying asphalt to finish her off.  We're all just plain ole men."

"Well, you're special to me."  Charlie blushed and gave a smile.

J.B. smiled proudly back, thought for a moment, then reached up, took off his hardhat and handed it to Charlie.  "Here kid, this is for you."

Charlie was nearly speechless.  The only thing he could muster was a "Wow!" and "Thank you!"

It began to rain.  Lighter at first and then harder.
J.B. got up to leave.  "See you around kid…"

Charlie felt the wetness on his cheeks as he awoke. It was a combination of the rain and George licking his face. Feeling disoriented, Charlie stood up. He looked around. Everything was in its right place, including the Mighty Mac.

As he got his bearings and turned to run to Grandma and Grandpa's house, he tripped over something. The hardhat!

Charlie bent down and picked it up. He thought for a moment, and then ran as fast as he could. He had to see his Grandpa!

The rain came down.

"Are we going to have to send a search party out after that grandson of yours?" Grandma was obviously getting worried. Charlie had been gone the whole afternoon. It was getting dark and was now raining very hard.

Just then Charlie, drenched, ran onto the porch and over to where his Grandma and Grandpa were standing.

"There you are," Grandma said with a sigh. "We have been worried about you."

With a polite, yet uninterested, wave of his hand, Charlie assured his Grandma that he was fine and went straight to his Grandpa's side.

"Fifty years ago we started work on the Mighty Mac and no one remembers," Grandpa announced. He seemed unaware of the fact that Charlie was dripping wet from head to toe, and was completely oblivious to the item he was holding in his hand.

"Thousands of men," Grandpa continued, "worked nearly non-stop for almost four years to change the way the people who travel this great state make their way between the two peninsulas. Is it being taken for granted?" Grandpa asked, not really expecting an answer.

"People remember, honey," Grandma tried to console. "They see that bridge and they are in awe. Always." And she hugged her husband.

"Fifty years, sonny boy."  Grandpa turned to Charlie.  "Fifty years since it all began."

And then, Charlie brought the hardhat into Grandpa's view.  "I remember, I know what it means to you."

Grandpa saw the hardhat, with his very own identifying union numbers on it, and could barely believe his eyes.

"Charlie, where in the world did you get that?  That's MY hardhat.  I gave it to a kid on the last day of the job."

"Come sit down, Grandpa, and I'll tell you."

"And Grandma, I think I have an idea for that history paper now," Charlie added.

The total suspension length of the Mackinac Bridge (including anchorages) is 8,614 feet making it the longest suspension bridge in the Western Hemisphere. Until 1998, when the Akashi Kaikyo Bridge in Japan (12,826 feet) and the Great Belt Bridge in Denmark (8,921 feet) were completed, the Mighty Mac held the title of longest in the world.

Thank you to the Mackinac Bridge Authority for the use of its extensive collection of archived photos.

Visit their website at www.mackinacbridge.org

Thank you Mr. Lawrence A. Rubin for your wealth of knowledge and chair at your table.

DATE DUE